The Solvit Kids

by Clara Mamet & Jack Quaid

A SAMUEL FRENCH ACTING EDITION

FOUNDED 1830

SAMUELFRENCH.COM

MUSIC USE NOTE

IMPORTANT BILLING AND CREDIT
REQUIREMENTS

THE SOLVIT KIDS opened in a world premiere production on April 13, 2012 at the Ruskin Group Theatre Company in Santa Monica, California. The evening of the two one acts was produced by John Ruskin, Artistic Director; Michael Meyers, Managing Director; and Mike Reilly, Production Manager. The production was directed by Paul Sand. The cast was as follows:

ANNIE WYATT . . . . Clara Mamet
BRADLEY PHILLIPS . . . . Sol Mason

CHARACTERS

BRADLEY PHILLIPS
ANNIE WYATT

(Two young people)

SET

Bradley's apartment: The room has a table and two chairs. A manuscript, a computer and a phone are set on top of the table. There is a couch, and a shelf with an urn resting on top of it. A window and a filing cabinet sit upstage and there is a cupboard next to the table.

(Bradley's apartment: **ANNIE** *and* **BRADLEY** *sit across from each other at a table.* **BRADLEY** *is on the phone.)*

BRADLEY. *(to phone)* Yes, Yes, Mr. Himmelman I understand, no no…no…that's fine, yes, yes, I realize that bu– yes but you see Mr. Himmelman, how was I supposed to know that–

ANNIE. *(to* **BRADLEY***)* Did you get rid of it?

BRADLEY. *(to* **ANNIE***)* One second, Annie *(to phone)* Mr. Himmelman…please do not speak to me that way, no, no, I'm so sorry…I will pay for it, absolutely I will pay for the damage, Mr. Himmelman, tomorrow I will have enough money to buy…to buy both your children, I can assure you I will be able to pay for the – no, I'm sorry, I'm sorry I didn't mean to offend you, I–

ANNIE. Did you get rid of it?

BRADLEY. *(to* **ANNIE***)* I – hold on, just one second. *(to phone)* Yes, Mr. Himmelman yes you are a very reasonable man and I will – certainly I will–

ANNIE. Did you–?

BRADLEY. *(to* **ANNIE***)* Yes, yes, I did, I put it in the incinerator its – *(to phone)* No, no Mr. Himmelman not your wife I was speaking to my – yes, yes, yes alright, I have to go but I will – yes, yes, I will be quiet, g'bye Mr. Himmelman. *(to* **ANNIE***)* I swear to god Annie, when I have money again I am going to book a room at the Ritz and then I am going to have that man killed. Do you know how long he has been alive? When I first got this place I was ten and he was ninety-six, it's–

ANNIE. Bradley focus, so for tomorrow, what about this: "Thank you, Ladies and Gentleman. Although it is under sad circumstances that my partner and I are reunited, we are proud to present a true literary genius' final work…"

BRADLEY. Whoa, wait a second.

ANNIE. What?

BRADLEY. You already wrote the speech?

ANNIE. No, that was just off the top of my head.

BRADLEY. Well, don't you think we should write it together?

ANNIE. We *are*, Bradley.

BRADLEY. Yeah, so don't finish half of it without me.

ANNIE. Okay, so what do you want to say?

BRADLEY. Uh...what did you say again?

ANNIE. Um..."It's under sad circumstances that my partner and I are reunited, but we..."

BRADLEY. That. I want to say that.

ANNIE. What? Just that one sentence?

BRADLEY. No that whole thing you said a second ago.

ANNIE. Okay...fine...

BRADLEY. We should have some sort of prop.

ANNIE. I think we should probably keep it simp–

(**BRADLEY** *looks to the shelf with the urn.*)

BRADLEY. What if I bring him?

ANNIE. You can't bring him.

BRADLEY. I feel like he would want to be there though.

ANNIE. No he wouldn't. Not like that.

BRADLEY. It's fine people will just think it's a vase.

ANNIE. There's no way they'll think it's a vase.

BRADLEY. I could put flowers in it.

ANNIE. In what? The urn?

BRADLEY. I'm just not sure if I feel like holding it all day? Ya'know its like it'll be sweet for the first few minutes but I have sensitive forearms and–

ANNIE. YOU CAN'T BRING THE ASHES BRADLEY!

(beat)

BRADLEY. Fine…

ANNIE. Alright, so…the speech–

BRADLEY. So what if I have a band give us some intro music...?

ANNIE. No.

BRADLEY. WHY N–

*(Phone rings. **BRADLEY** answers.)*

BRADLEY. *(on phone)* Hello? Hi Mr. Himmelman...Yeah...I– no I don't think that is a rule of our apartment complex. No...no, we are allowed to have members of the opposite sex in our rooms. Well – I don't see how that – she's, no, she's not a prostitute. Well sir, I'm afraid you've got me there sir because I don't know what a "nancy boy" is! Yes – yes, alright, I'll be quiet, I'm being quiet...we'll try and be quiet. *(**BRADLEY** hangs up.)* Well first I think the band should play "Eye of the Ti..."

ANNIE. NO we're not–

BRADLEY. We should start with a quote from the book.

ANNIE. Why don't we type out a speech?

BRADLEY. "Only love can break the spell, only time can heal the wound."

ANNIE. You can wear your nice Brooks Brothers suit, and I'll–

BRADLEY. On the day, you should give me a heads up before you start to weep, and I could hold on to your chin or something and say–

ANNIE. Why don't we write just both write a list of all the things that were nice about him, and we can take turns reading them aloud–

BRADLEY. What if we come in full costume?

ANNIE. I don't think you get it, Bradley...

BRADLEY. I mean if we're going back to work in a few months I think it might be a comfort to know that the costumes still fit.

ANNIE. Uh, Brad...

BRADLEY. I would like people to use the word "shebang" when they look back on this event, I don't think that's too much to–

ANNIE. Bradley...

BRADLEY. Why don't we open with the first line of the new book. That'd be cute, right? Be like a little teaser? Read it to me real quick.

ANNIE. No.

BRADLEY. Please?

ANNIE. No.

BRADLEY. Please?

ANNIE. No.

BRADLEY. PLEASE?

ANNIE. FINE

BRADLEY. PLEASE?!

ANNIE. I SAID FINE.

BRADLEY. Thank you.

(ANNIE takes the manuscript that is on the table and removes the ribbon that is tied around it.)

ANNIE. Ugh...all right here we go... *(reading)* "The Solvit Kids Book Seven: Chapter One: The second time my uncle molested me; I realized I liked it..."

(long beat)

BRADLEY. What?

ANNIE. That can't be a correct thing...

BRADLEY. No...

ANNIE. It has to be a printing error or something right?

BRADLEY. Yeah, of course. It's probably just a printing error.

ANNIE. This is just irresponsible.

BRADLEY. Yeah uh...flip around a little...that could just be the wrong part.

ANNIE. Yeah but...okay...uh...

BRADLEY. Oh! Check the end! Did we finally defeat Count Dizionario?

ANNIE. *(flipping through)* Uh...I don't... He's not mentioned. I don't even see anything about the wizard of Olmur.

BRADLEY. What? He was a major character in the last book.

ANNIE. I know! But Bradley I don't even see anything about John and Jane.

BRADLEY. What? Well check the last line! I always have the last line!

ANNIE. Okay...

(ANNIE *looks to the back of the manuscript. Beat.*)

ANNIE. It says, "Disregard the Jews."

BRADLEY. That doesn't sound like something John Solvit would say.

ANNIE. I don't think your character even says this.

BRADLEY. WHAT? I always say the last line! Go back a little. Maybe that's the epilogue or something?

ANNIE. These books never have epilogues.

BRADLEY. Whatever just check the middle. Does it say anything about our missing father or Mrs. Moss?

ANNIE. This doesn't sound like a Solvit book.

BRADLEY. Maybe they're taking it in a darker direction? I don't know.

ANNIE. Maybe they gave us the wrong thing?

BRADLEY. All I see are the words orphan and arousal–

ANNIE. I can't believe this is happening...

BRADLEY. He spelled "douche" wrong.

ANNIE. Oh my god. Brad?

BRADLEY. What?

ANNIE. What did the will say?

BRADLEY. Uh...burn the book with the mauve string, the one with the lilac string I leave to you.

ANNIE. No...no it didn't, it said burn the book with the lilac string, the one with the mauve string I... What the hell is mauve?

BRADLEY. It's like a type of light purple. I think. It's like lilac!

ANNIE. But what is lilac, Bradley?

BRADLEY. A different shade of light purple? I think? I don't know!

ANNIE. So what did you just burn?

(*beat*)

BRADLEY. Oh dear god.

ANNIE. OH MY GOD!!!!

BRADLEY. Oh my god…

ANNIE. How did we get them confused?

BRADLEY. WHAT'S LILAC!!!

ANNIE. I don't know!

BRADLEY. Jesus Christ!

ANNIE. Do you know what we just did, Bradley?

BRADLEY. I KNOW!!!!

ANNIE. DO YOU KNOW HOW MUCH MONEY IS IN THAT INCINERATOR?

BRADLEY. Probably a lot!

ANNIE. How are we going to explain this to…?

BRADLEY. America?

ANNIE. Oh God!

BRADLEY. What?

ANNIE. The press conference…

BRADLEY. Oh my god!!!!!

ANNIE. What the hell are we going to give them?

BRADLEY. What the hell is lilac?

ANNIE. All right, all right. Let me just look at the…

BRADLEY. I mean those were horrible instructions!

ANNIE. JUST!!! JUST!!! It's all right. Hold on. Let me just read…

(**ANNIE** *looks down at the manuscript.*)

ANNIE. (*reading*) "My wife thinks I'm gay, I disagree."

(beat)

ANNIE. What is this?!?!

BRADLEY. STOP ASKING ME!

ANNIE. WHAT ARE WE GOING TO DO.

BRADLEY. STOP. YELLING.

ANNIE. Okay, okay you're right...we just have to make a plan.

*(Beat. **BRADLEY** looks at the manuscript.)*

BRADLEY. Annie?

ANNIE. Shut up.

BRADLEY. Annie...

ANNIE. WHAT?

BRADLEY. It says Memorandum on the cover.

ANNIE. Oh, Jesus Christ...JESUS CHRIST that's perfect OF COURSE these are his memoirs.

BRADLEY. Whose? His?

ANNIE. Yes.

BRADLEY. Why would he want them burned? On the other hand–

ANNIE. What are we going to do, Brad?

BRADLEY. Well, I suppose there's nothing we *can* do.

*(**BRADLEY** grabs the phone and dials 411.)*

ANNIE. What are you doing?

BRADLEY. It's alright – Me and the publisher are old friends.

ANNIE. That's not what I'm thinking about!

BRADLEY. Annie, it's alright I can get us another copy of the book if you'll just let me–

ANNIE. Wait a minute...

BRADLEY. Shhhh...

ANNIE. We don't have to tell them.

BRADLEY. Annie, I'm on the phone please be...

ANNIE. Don't do that!

*(**ANNIE** tries to grab the phone. **BRADLEY** holds it away from her.)*

BRADLEY. Calm down – I'm just…

ANNIE. STOP IT!

BRADLEY. You really need to relax.

(**ANNIE** *finally gets hold of the phone and hangs up.*)

BRADLEY. What are you doing?

ANNIE. I will not be cheated of my fortune.

(*She grabs Bradley's computer.*)

BRADLEY. What?

ANNIE. We gotta write it, Brad.

BRADLEY. Huh?

ANNIE. We're gonna write "The Solvit Kids: Book 7."

BRADLEY. We can't write the book! We just burned the book!

ANNIE. Exactly that's why we're writing the book.

BRADLEY. But it's his book. This is like theft.

ANNIE. It's not theft, if anything it's charity.

BRADLEY. Annie, seriously you're over–reacting. There's gotta be another copy somewhere, if you'll just let me…

ANNIE. BRAD! He used to handwrite the books out on a scroll like the Torah, do you remember when the second book went to print he wept for weeks, went on a gigantic boozer and they found him a month later in Montreal with a mail-order bride. What about him would ever give you the indication that he made copies?

BRADLEY. How can you say that in front of him?

(**BRADLEY** *points towards the urn.*)

ANNIE. Are you kidding me?

BRADLEY. Annie, seriously. I don't think it's appropriate for you to write in his name. I mean these things take time and years of experience. I heard he was working on the seventh book for two years. This isn't the sort of thing you can do in a day!

ANNIE. Okay in "The Solvit Kids Book 7: the Mystery of the Jade Dragon," Jane and John travel to China to figure out why the local peasant's crops have died. They find themselves entangled in a web of international intrigue and with the help of a scrappy young monk they uncover the secrets of the mysterious Jade Dragon: A ghost ship that mysteriously disappeared centuries ago. Turns out that Count Dizionario is behind it all somehow, whatever. Mrs. Moss turns out to be their mother. They don't know how to break the spell, but they look inside themselves and realize that that is enough. Yada. Yada. Yada...and at the end John says...

BRADLEY. "And just in time for supper?"

ANNIE. RIGHT! And everyone goes home happy, having learned more about themselves.

(beat)

BRADLEY. That's amazing. Did he tell you that before he died?

ANNIE. NO Brad! That was just off the top of my head!

BRADLEY. Have you ever considered writing? 'Cause that was...

ANNIE. Brad have you ever actually *read* the books? The formula's the same every time. Anyone could write these books. They're awful.

BRADLEY. How can you say that?

ANNIE. In every book John and Jane travel to a far off land to solve a problem. They solve it. Count Dizionario is behind it all. The peasants they save thank them with regional foods and Jane gets her period for the first time. In every. Single. Book.

BRADLEY. That isn't...

ANNIE. It's not just me. The entire world knows these books are a joke.

BRADLEY. That's not true!

ANNIE. Yes it is.

BRADLEY. No it's not.

ANNIE. Yes it IS…these books are ridiculous–

BRADLEY. Why can't you just enjoy being the front of a phenomenon! You're Jane Solvit for god sakes!

ANNIE. Not anymore, Brad!

BRADLEY. What?

(beat)

ANNIE. Oh god you really don't know. Do you?

BRADLEY. What?

ANNIE. We're not going to be in the movie.

BRADLEY. What?

ANNIE. Brad, the last one was made like ten years ago.

BRADLEY. …So?

ANNIE. Well, you didn't think you'd still pass for ten did you?

BRADLEY. Well, I thought…

ANNIE. Listen, we're finally getting paid off for the most embarrassing years of our lives…enjoy it.

BRADLEY. No…

ANNIE. Wha'dyou mean "no?"

BRADLEY. This can't be happening to me…

ANNIE. Bradley, hold on a second.

BRADLEY. How…DARE THEY!

ANNIE. Hang on a minute…

BRADLEY. No, no, you know what? They can't just spring this on me like this…they can't just…look, look there…see that?

*(**BRADLEY** takes out an old newspaper clipping from his pocket and holds it up to **ANNIE**.)*

ANNIE. Your headshot?

BRADLEY. No, no not just my…the article, the article, look at the second par…

ANNIE. Bradley, listen to me…

BRADLEY. You see that article?

ANNIE. Yeah.

BRADLEY. Have you read it?

ANNIE. No, and please don't…

BRADLEY. *(reading)* "Hollywood's hottest actor, Bradley Phillips (John Solvit, Solvit series…) came to talk to us today about his latest role in the sixth Solvit film. As he walked into the restaurant sporting cut–up jeans and a flannel tank, we could see that Hollywood's young stud is surprisingly down-to-earth for someone so famous."

ANNIE. Bradley…

BRADLEY. 'I like to experiment physically with the role as I delve deeper into the soul of John Solvit,' Says Phillips, who is quite mature for an eleven year…"

ANNIE. How old is that article–

BRADLEY. That's not the point!

ANNIE. It's been ten years!

BRADLEY. No one can do John Solvit better than me!

ANNIE. I know that and you know that….but the public is going to be confused when..

BRADLEY. I can play a fifth–grader.

ANNIE. YOU'RE TWENTY ONE!

    (beat)

    Look it's all right. I know you miss it but there'll be other movies. And…and wait what's that show you're on again?

BRADLEY. *Beach Cops: New York…*

ANNIE. *Beach Cops: New York!* Wow! I mean that's…that's great.

BRADLEY. Thank you…

    (beat)

ANNIE. Brad, I'm sorry. Are you okay?

BRADLEY. It's just, no one told me anything.

ANNIE. They never tell you anything, Brad.

BRADLEY. It just isn't right. You work your whole life and then one day some kid just thinks he can walk into the room from, I don't know, Tampa, and steal the show?

ANNIE. Listen okay! ENOUGH!!! You love this series, right?

BRADLEY. Yeah.

ANNIE. So wouldn't you want to see it end well?

BRADLEY. I guess so.

ANNIE. So let's write this thing!!!!

BRADLEY. Honestly I'm just a little uncomfortable writing someone else's book.

ANNIE. Do you want that money?

BRADLEY. It's not the money, Annie. It's the principle of the thing.

ANNIE. You're going to turn down billions of dollars on principle?

BRADLEY. Yes.

ANNIE. Yes?

BRADLEY. Yeah this just isn't right.

ANNIE. Do you know what will happen to you? If millions of little kids find out that you burned the last "Solvit" book?

BRADLEY. What do you mean?

ANNIE. You'd never work in this town again. You walk away from this and you can you can kiss *Beach Cops* good-bye my friend.

(beat)

BRADLEY. Alright...

ANNIE. Alright, great. Excellent. So what were we doing at the end of the last book?

*(**ANNIE** opens the computer and begins to type.)*

BRADLEY. Wait we need a title first.

ANNIE. "They Mystery of the Jade Dragon."

BRADLEY. Love it.

ANNIE. Great so what were we doing at the end of the last book?

BRADLEY. Uh... we had just stopped Count Dizionario from polluting imp–fairy lake.

ANNIE. Ugh...okay... So every book starts with...

BRADLEY. We get called out of class by Mrs. Moss, our principal slash boss to go out on an assignment.

ANNIE. Yeah, what really is she?

BRADLEY. I don't know.

ANNIE. Okay so we're studying...

BRADLEY. ...ancient Chinese...

ANNIE. ...cultures or whatever, and that's going to help them later to...

BRADLEY. ...find the Jade Dragon.

ANNIE. Okay so Mrs. Moss comes over the loudspeaker and she's like, "Will Jane and John Solvit please come to the principal's office?" and then we go...

BRADLEY. Don't forget: Everybody in the classroom thinks we're in trouble.

ANNIE. Okay, they all go "ooo."

BRADLEY. Mhm

ANNIE. Okay, so...

BRADLEY. Read that back to me.

ANNIE. All right, *(reading)* "It was a dreary day for the Solvit kids as they sat in their third period social studies class. They were learning about ancient Chinese dragons. Particularly, Jade ones..."

BRADLEY. Nice.

ANNIE. "When suddenly a firm but kindly voice came over the loudspeaker: 'Will Jane and John Solvit please report to the principal's office?' Their classmates snickered to themselves. It would seem as if..."

BRADLEY. Don't forget the "ooo."

*(**ANNIE** hits delete a few times.)*

ANNIE. "It would seem as if they we're going 'ooo.'"

BRADLEY. Yes.

ANNIE. So, "As they walked the long walk to Mrs. Moss' office..."

BRADLEY. Wait we have to establish my street smarts...

ANNIE. ..."John knew exactly how to get there!"

BRADLEY. Yes.

ANNIE. Okay so, *(really fast)* "They walked the walk and John knew exactly how to get there." *(back to normal pace)* "This walk that they walked was..."

BRADLEY. Pensive?

ANNIE. "Because they were thinking so much about what..."

BRADLEY. Thinking so much about what the mission could be.

ANNIE. Yeah, "Suddenly from behind a locker appeared Melinda: The most popular girl in school, and if my readers remember correctly..."

BRADLEY. I have an idea.

ANNIE. "...was John's old flame..." What?

BRADLEY. What if...we're in college?

(beat)

ANNIE. ...No?

BRADLEY. What if it's the Solvit Kids at twenty.

ANNIE. That doesn't make any sense.

BRADLEY. No, no, no what if it's set like ten years later? And Mrs. Moss is now our *dean* slash boss?

ANNIE. But every book always picked up where the last one ended, what have we been doing for ten years?

BRADLEY. UH...OKAY!!!! Annie, this is great. They got caught in a time warp made by count Dizionario and now...they have to go to freshman orientation!!!!

ANNIE. No, Bradley.

BRADLEY. C'mon it's brilliant! That's what people want to see these days anyway right? College sex comedies?

ANNIE. You have to let this go.

BRADLEY. Please?

ANNIE. Uh.... "If my readers remember correctly was John's old flame..."

BRADLEY. Okay now she's a sexy cheerleader that all the guys want to...

ANNIE. "Melinda walked down the hall...and completely ignored John."

BRADLEY. What? No.

ANNIE. Listen. We have... (ANNIE *checks her watch.*) Eight hours! We're not going to be able to do this if you keep nagging me.

BRADLEY. Fine...

ANNIE. Okay so Melinda ignores John...

BRADLEY. John ignores Melinda and we go into Mrs. Moss' office right?

ANNIE. Right. Great. "They entered Mrs. Moss' office...

BRADLEY. ...slash cottage.

ANNIE. Right "slash cottage and her faithful receptionist told them that she would be right with them. She–

BRADLEY. Hold on.

ANNIE. What?

BRADLEY. I have an idea...

ANNIE. What?

BRADLEY. We're in high school...

ANNIE. Oh my god.

BRADLEY. ...and someone's been poisoning the cafeteria food. He calls himself, BUM BUM BUM, the Jade Dragon!

ANNIE. Stop it.

BRADLEY. OH! And here we go. Get this...Mrs. Moss is the LUNCH LADY!!!!

ANNIE. BRADLEY, FOR THE LOVE OF GOD, SHUT UP!

BRADLEY. Or maybe it could be their chem teacher that's experimenting with jade in the hopes of altering the minds of the SAT examiners!

ANNIE. The Solvit Kids are nine and ten. Your catchphrase is "and just in time for supper." That's not even a full sentence, you CAN'T be a twenty-one year old adult.

(**BRADLEY** *grabs the manuscript and starts flipping through it.*)

BRADLEY. But wait didn't his memoirs say that he liked the fact that the young could be older, or there was youngness in everyone or something? That age wasn't particularly a factor and that–

ANNIE. He was a pedophile, Bradley.

BRADLEY. Huh?

ANNIE. He was a raging pedophile...

(*beat*)

BRADLEY. No he wasn't.

ANNIE. Uh...yeah he was.

BRADLEY. "Raging?"

ANNIE. Brad, this was something *everyone* knew.

BRADLEY. Oh... (*beat*) That's...

ANNIE. Look, I know I've hit you with a lot of bombshells today...

BRADLEY. That's...

ANNIE. But if you can just look past it for now...

BRADLEY. That's...PERFECT!!!

ANNIE. What?

(**BRADLEY** *puts his finger on a page and starts to read.*)

BRADLEY. Annie, shut up and listen to this, "My father was a stern man. He would beat me with a belt every time I came home with a good report card. He took me to Dr. Jamieson several times due to an injured rectum. I always blamed it the uncomfortable chair in our living room, but something told me he knew."

ANNIE. What about it?

BRADLEY. "What about it?" It's amazing! I mean anyone could relate to this.

ANNIE. Are you gay?

BRADLEY. You're missing the point!

ANNIE. Am I though?

BRADLEY. Look at this! This is cinematic genius! His life is chock full of these rich dramatic moments.

ANNIE. Wow... You're taking this pedophile thing really well.

(He flips through the memoirs vigorously.)

BRADLEY. Look; molestations, beatings, stealing clothes, literary success, alcoholism, and wait... CANCER? ARE YOU KIDDING? THIS IS GOLD!!!

ANNIE. How can everyone relate to that? When have you ever experienced *any* of those things? You grew up in the Palisades and went to boarding school in New Hampshire.

BRADLEY. You don't have to have experienced something to relate to it.

ANNIE. Yes...actually you do.

BRADLEY. Well the tables are about to turn!!!

ANNIE. What are you talking about?

BRADLEY. I have an idea, Annie...

ANNIE. What?

BRADLEY. THIS!

ANNIE. What?

BRADLEY. We pitch this to the studio and make a movie of his life. I play him. BAM! We're back!

ANNIE. No, absolutely not.

BRADLEY. AND YOU! You could play... *(BRADLEY looks to a random page.)*

ANNIE. I don't care. Listen, Brad...

(He finds a part for her.)

BRADLEY. You could play, PATTY! His nanny for two years!

ANNIE. I really don't care. Listen...

BRADLEY. No YOU listen, this is fate. The book is gone! *The Solvit Kids* are terrible anyway, you said it yourself.

ANNIE. Yeah, but this is just disgusting.

BRADLEY. C'mon we'll get our movie careers back! Here I'll call Ken right now.

ANNIE. NO, NOT KEN, It's not going to sell, Brad.

BRADLEY. I disagree.

ANNIE. Quality aside, you can't just take away *The Solvit Kids* and give the people... *(She reads the first line of the memoirs again.)* "The second time my uncle molested me I realized I liked it." They'll kill us Brad. And what's more, you'll soil his name forever. Nobody's going to want the read *The Solvit Kids* if they were written by... this. I mean we haven't even read through the whole thing yet. He could've been a Nazi for all we know.

BRADLEY. EVEN BETTER – you know what? Just hold on a second, let me try something.

(BRADLEY closes his eyes and places his fingers on his temples.)

ANNIE. What are you doing?

BRADLEY. SHHH!

(Beat. BRADLEY begins to do an improvised monologue.)

Mother? Mother is that you? I know things haven't been the same since he took to the drink but he's a good man. Although he beats me, he treats me with respect and dignity, always. Also, Mother. I'm going to be a college man. Mr. Collins said he would pay for Harvard if I did some things around his house. Sweeping, dusting, and having sex with him. Sometimes I resist, the sex that is, but I know it's for the greater good.

ANNIE. Please stop that.

BRADLEY. Don't you see the potential here?

ANNIE. No. Sit down. Where were we?

BRADLEY. You were trying to come up with a witty retort but you couldn't 'cause you lack artistic perception!

ANNIE. Brad, calm down!

BRADLEY. You don't care about what I want at all do you?

ANNIE. Bradley!!!

BRADLEY. You're so selfish!

ANNIE. You're being ridiculous!

BRADLEY. You didn't give it a chance!

ANNIE. Where were we?

BRADLEY. Ugh...

ANNIE. WHERE WERE WE?

BRADLEY. We were in the office, and you were gonna say a retort!

ANNIE. Oh, yeah so you say, "We haven't heard that before", And I say...

BRADLEY. This is stupid.

ANNIE. Stop complaining. You're being a baby.

BRADLEY. I'm not being a baby! You're being close-minded.

ANNIE. Ugh...okay so we go into her office, and she gives us our assignment.

BRADLEY. I want to bring him to the press conference!

ANNIE. You can't bring ashes to a press conference!

BRADLEY. Why?

ANNIE. It's not something people do!

BRADLEY. It's original!

ANNIE. We have to go to China because...

BRADLEY. They want us to be judges in a wet T-shirt contest!

ANNIE. NO!!!

BRADLEY. But it's spring break!

ANNIE. They're not in college!

BRADLEY. Why not?!?!?!?

ANNIE. Brad. You can't be in the movie. It's over okay?

BRADLEY. NO!!!!! It's not over!!!! It's NEVER OVER!!!!!! OKAY?!

(**BRADLEY** *flings the computer across the room. It breaks.*)

ANNIE. Brad, what the hell?

(*phone rings*)

BRADLEY. (*on the phone*) Yes, hello, hi Mr. Himmelman, yes, I know I'm very sorry…I am so sorry we will keep the noise down, but if you'll excuse me now, I'm a little bit upset and I have to dea– excuse me sir, I will not be spoken to like that I will have you know that I am an actor on an extremely reputable TV show – and what is wrong with *Beach Cops?*

ANNIE. (*over* **BRADLEY**) You just destroyed everything!!!!

BRADLEY. We're giving them the memoirs, Annie. Trust me you'll thank me later. (*to phone*) Bye Mr. Himmelman.

ANNIE. And what exactly are you planning to do?

(**BRADLEY** *hangs up the phone and redials.*)

BRADLEY. (*to phone*) Hello, can I please be connected to Random House Publishing, yes *again.*

ANNIE. YOU CAN'T DO THAT!

BRADLEY. I'm gonna do you one better, I'm telling him we burned the book.

ANNIE. YOU BURNED THE BOOK.

BRADLEY. That's immaterial, and it's happening!!!

ANNIE. GIVE ME BACK THE PHONE!

BRADLEY. (*to phone*) Hello is that Ken I hear?

ANNIE. NO!!!

(**ANNIE** *grabs for the phone and they wrestle for it.*)

ANNIE. It's not going to sell Brad!!

(**ANNIE** *rips the phone out of his hands. She hits the end button.*)

Listen to me!

BRADLEY. Give that back!

ANNIE. I have an idea!

BRADLEY. I don't care!

(**BRADLEY** *attempts to grab the phone.*)

ANNIE. Hear me out for a second!

BRADLEY. WHAT?

ANNIE. I'll make you a deal.

BRADLEY. I'm listening...

ANNIE. You can do the memoirs.

BRADLEY. Great! Now give me back my...

ANNIE. BUT! You have to help me with this book first!

BRADLEY. What? No!

ANNIE. Think about it. You can use the profits from the book to fund your movie.

BRADLEY. I don't want to use my own money!

ANNIE. Okay, we'll only give them *The Solvit Kids* if they'll back the movie! You can even direct it Brad!

BRADLEY. Really?

ANNIE. Yeah you can do whatever you want with it. I don't care. You just need to help me write this first!

(*beat*)

BRADLEY. I don't trust this...

ANNIE. Okay, here! What if we announce your movie at the press conference? You'll have publicity before it's even a screenplay.

BRADLEY. Okay...

ANNIE. Okay?

BRADLEY. Okay.

ANNIE. Great... Are you done?

(*beat*)

BRADLEY. Yes.

ANNIE. Wonderful.

BRADLEY. But what are we going to write this with?

ANNIE. You should have thought of that before you threw the computer.

BRADLEY. You know what, Annie? Immature, alright? Pointing fingers is not going to–

ANNIE. Wait hold on!

BRADLEY. What?

(She reaches into her purse and pulls out a notepad, along with a pen.)

ANNIE. There we go!

BRADLEY. Won't it take longer to write it by hand?

ANNIE. This'll be better. It'll look more authentic!

BRADLEY. Whatever.

*(**ANNIE** begins to write in her notebook.)*

ANNIE. Alright. So Mrs. Moss gives them their assignment to go to China and find out why the peasants' crops are dying...

BRADLEY. Mhm...

ANNIE. Then we cut to...

BRADLEY. US ON A PLANE!!!!

ANNIE. And then we cut to

BRADLEY. Us landing the plane.

ANNIE. And then we cut to–

BRADLEY. China airport.

ANNIE. And then, we make a friend. And then–

BRADLEY. His name is PACO! And then–

ANNIE. We go to the sea!

BRADLEY. Great! Then the pirates take us captive! There is an evil plan.

ANNIE. YES!

BRADLEY. What is his evil plan?

ANNIE. Unimportant.

BRADLEY. Yeah, then we walk the plank.

ANNIE. YEAH! They leave us for dead because of the blood.

BRADLEY. Yeap. But we're not.

ANNIE. Nope.

BRADLEY. Because the blood is just–

ANNIE. JANE'S PERIOD.

BRADLEY. YES!

ANNIE. And then the Solvits emerge victorious! And the peasants have a feast to–

BRADLEY. Celebrate Jane's WOMANHOOD!

ANNIE. YES! AND THAT'S WHEN YOU SAY–

BRADLEY. "And just in time for supper!"

ANNIE. BAM!!!

BRADLEY. DONE!!!!

(beat)

ANNIE. I'm out of ink.

BRADLEY. Well don't you have another?

ANNIE. No...

BRADLEY. Why not?

ANNIE. I didn't expect to be writing an entire book today! What you don't have pens in your house?

BRADLEY. No I don't...

ANNIE. Who are you?

BRADLEY. Somebody else always has the pen. I'm a pen borrower, not an owner. Besides, I have a computer.

ANNIE. You broke the computer.

BRADLEY. *Had* a computer, I had no need for pens.

ANNIE. Why don't you just run to the store?

BRADLEY. It's three in the morning, Annie. I doubt "Staples" is open. **(BRADLEY** *motions to Annie's purse.)* Well is there anything else in there we could write with?

(ANNIE looks in her bag again and takes out some liquid eyeliner.)

BRADLEY. Eyeliner?

ANNIE. It's the only thing I have.

BRADLEY. Okay...

(**ANNIE** *goes to continue writing and* **BRADLEY** *grabs the eyeliner and notebook out of her hand.*)

I'll write it, I aced Calligraphy in high school.

ANNIE. Okay, but just be careful.

BRADLEY. Okay I got it.

ANNIE. Seriously, though, Brad PLEASE make the rest of the book fit on that thing, I don't have anything else.

BRADLEY. Alright, I got it, I got it…

(productive writing silence)

BRADLEY. Annie?

ANNIE. Yeah?

BRADLEY. It appears that your makeup is extremely liquidy and I started to draw a picture, which I realize now was probably ill-advised. Also I'm pretty sure it bled through the rest of your notebook.

(He holds up the notebook to reveal the entire thing has been soaked in liquid eyeliner.)

ANNIE. OH MY GOD!

BRADLEY. Okay, just calm down! Alright? We'll think of something…

ANNIE. No we won't….

BRADLEY. YES! YES! We will, it's gonna be fine, I have an idea.

(**BRADLEY** *goes to the filing cabinet and pulls out a stack of old scripts.*)

ANNIE. What are those?

(**BRADLEY** *puts the scripts down on the table.*)

BRADLEY. These are *Beach Cops* Annie! The FULL series completely at our disposal.

ANNIE. Well at least now we have some more paper…

BRADLEY. Annie, please, what a ridiculous suggestion, I'm not soiling these with our *fake prose*, we're searching these for clues.

ANNIE. For clues?

BRADLEY. Just trust me.

*(**BRADLEY** and **ANNIE** start flipping through old copies of "Beach Cops".)*

BRADLEY. Okay…what does yours say?

ANNIE. I really don't think this is going to help us, Brad.

BRADLEY. Okay, well I don't think your giving it enough credit, and your also not looking in the right places… for example…Oh okay this is great… as you probably remember as this is episode #312…

ANNIE. Nope.

BRADLEY. The beach cops are trapped underground and use coffee grinds to scribble a note.

ANNIE. Why would a note help you in that situation…?

BRADLEY. Okay, can you stop asking irrelevant questions? Don't you see?! This is brilliant!

ANNIE. It is?

BRADLEY. Yeah, okay…go get some coffee grinds from the cupboard and mix them up in a bowl.

ANNIE. Coffee grinds?

BRADLEY. Yes!

ANNIE. To write with?

BRADLEY. Yes!

ANNIE. How?

BRADLEY. We'll put them in this!

*(**BRADLEY** takes out an enormous quill that was under the table.)*

ANNIE. Why do you have that?

BRADLEY. It was on sale.

ANNIE. Alright fine, sure…that'll work but why don't you make the coffee grind solution and I'll just.

*(**ANNIE** reaches for all the Beach Cops scripts.)*

BRADLEY. What are you doing?

ANNIE. What?

BRADLEY. What are you doing with *Beach Cops?*

ANNIE. Well, we need to write on the back of them.

BRADLEY. No.

ANNIE. Oh, Bradley come on, we need to use them will you please hand them to me so we can–

BRADLEY. NO!

ANNIE. We have no choice, what else would we–

BRADLEY. I have an idea.

ANNIE. Your idea is stupid.

BRADLEY. You haven't even heard it…

ANNIE. It's going to be stupid…

BRADLEY. What if…

ANNIE. No…

BRADLEY. What if…we make a potato print.

ANNIE. A potato print? You mean like a stamp…

BRADLEY. Yes! You know…you print something backwards on a potato. Dip it in some coffee grinds…smudge it on the page…it reads just like a regular sentence and you're good to go!

ANNIE. You want to make a stamp of a novel.

BRADLEY. Yes!

ANNIE. NO!

BRADLEY. Well it doesn't have to be a potato…

ANNIE. Alright…

BRADLEY. It can be a melon…

ANNIE. What?

BRADLEY. WE can etch it into a melon instead.

ANNIE. Bradley…it's not the type of surface that we etch it onto…it's the actual etching process I am concerned about!

BRADLEY. What does that mean?

ANNIE. You are going to etch a full length children's novel into a melon?

BRADLEY. …You're right…you're right. *(beat)* It should be a potato,

ANNIE. NO! You're missing the point! No...we are not going to do any etching of any kind, we are simply going to dip this enormous quill into watered down coffee grinds and print it on the back of these scripts!

BRADLEY. No.

ANNIE. PLEASE?

BRADLEY. Absolutely not.

ANNIE. Brad, why do you want to keep all these, they're from – I don't even know, and they're not doing much–

BRADLEY. Excuse me I read these to my grandmother while she was dying, thank you very much.

ANNIE. Did she ask you to do that?

BRADLEY. Not the point–it's, it's sentimental it really is, and what's more–

ANNIE. Look at how much paper it is, we REALLY NEED it Brad, we're SO CLOSE, CAN YOU PLEASE?!

BRADLEY. My grandmother wouldn't want it.

ANNIE. YOUR GRANDMOTHER WOULDN'T CARE!

BRADLEY. HER LAST WORDS WERE, "NEVER TOO OLD TO BE BACK AT THE BEACH BOYS, STAY STRONG, CARRY ON, AND I'LL SEE YOU IN THE CABANA MONDAY."

ANNIE. THAT'S BECAUSE YOU WERE MAKING HER RUN LINES WITH YOU!!!

BRADLEY. REGARDLESS OF THE SITUATION! IT'S–

ANNIE. YOURE NOT LISTENING!

BRADLEY. I AM SO LISTENING AND I DON'T WANT TO...IT WOULD BE DISRESPECTFUL TO GRANNY.

(beat)

ANNIE. Brad...you're right...you're so right...what I said before, I was wrong...of course your grandmother loved the series. She loved your work. She was running lines with you ON HER DEATH BED because she loved your work so much–

BRADLEY. But I thought you said that–

ANNIE: Everyone says things they don't mean when they're angry...Listen Brad, your grandmother DIED hearing your acting...in a way, your career was what her life was all about – don't you think you owe it to her memory to write on these manuscripts. You must write on them for the greater good...For a new project has arisen! Death and Rebirth! Just...it's just like your grandmother symbolizes...

BRADLEY. My grandmother symbolizes death and rebirth?

ANNIE. Are you talking shit about your grandma?

BRADLEY. No! I love Nana, I–

ANNIE. Are you telling me that you won't write a new book on the backs of the scripts she loved 'cause you don't want her to be happy?

BRADLEY. No, no...wait now, now I'm confused...I...

ANNIE. You think you're better than your grandma? Cause let me tell you something...your grandma was a fine, fine lady, and writing on the back of these scripts would be the greatest honor you could do to her memory and if you don't–

BRADLEY. Wait, hold on...lemme just think about this for a second.

ANNIE. Do this for us! Let's...let's make this happen! You will be using these for the greater good not only of your grandmother, but of this project, the world will have the *Solvit* series, right? And you will feel good because you have done a good deed...NO NO you will feel good because you will be helping – helping your MOVIE!

(**ANNIE** *can see* **BRADLEY** *has perked up at this.*)

We need to finish this so you can do your movie – do it for your movie.

(*phone rings*)

BRADLEY. (*to phone*) WHAT IS IT – (*lowering his voice*) I'm sorry Mr. Himmelman what can I do for – yes, yes, we will try and keep the noise level – yes, No, No please don't call the police I'm very sorry it won't happen again. (**BRADLEY** *hangs up. Long beat.*) Okay…Okay… Okay…I'll do it.

ANNIE. Oh, good…

*(**ANNIE** goes to the cupboard to get the coffee grinds.)*

BRADLEY. Anyway I'm so glad I had those.

*(**ANNIE** takes them off the shelf. She weighs them in the palm of her hand. Beat.)*

ANNIE. Hey Brad.

BRADLEY. Yeah?

ANNIE. There's no coffee in here.

BRADLEY. Oh that's right.

ANNIE. What do you mean, "Oh that's right."

BRADLEY. Well, I forgot…

ANNIE. Forgot what, exactly?

BRADLEY. I used it all…

ANNIE. On what?

(beat)

BRADLEY. A potato print experiment.

ANNIE. Oh, good.

BRADLEY. It didn't really work…that's why I had to use so much.

ANNIE. Why would you have suggested that if it didn't work in the first place?

BRADLEY. I don't know…I just thought…

ANNIE. Oh Brad…

BRADLEY. I'm really sorry…I

ANNIE. OH JESUS CHRIST JUST SHUT UP FOR A MINUTE

(beat)

Okay…I have it.

BRADLEY. Have what?

ANNIE. Bring him to me.

(**ANNIE** *motions to the urn.*)

BRADLEY. Why?

ANNIE. Well…we're all out of coffee…

BRADLEY. OH No…NO…NO, ABSOLUTELY NOT!

ANNIE. KAY WELL, I'M NOT THE ONE WHO USED UP ALL MY COFFEE GRINDS TO MAKE UNSUCESSFULL POTATO PRINTS, ALRIGHT?

BRADLEY. No…ANNIE…NO! *Beach Cops* is one thing, but this?

ANNIE. What about this irks you more…

BRADLEY. Well…where am I going to say I put them?

ANNIE. Over the Brooklyn Bridge? In his hometown, I don't–

BRADLEY. I don't have a very good feeling about–

ANNIE. Don't you see the beauty of it, Brad? He left them to you so where you spread them is entirely at your discress–

BRADLEY. This is crazy, its crazy, its just–

ANNIE. Well…they're expecting you to spread his ashes anyway, and he might be happy to know that he participated in this…endeavor. And like you said, it's not like anyone would know…

BRADLEY. Annie, Annie, I can't – You're making me uncomfortable and–

ANNIE. Think about it as an homage to him.

BRADLEY. Its not an homage it's a sacrifice!

ANNIE. Its both! Isn't it beautiful, and when its all over you can use it as an inspiration for the biopic and–

BRADLEY. I can't, I can't, I'm, I'm, Its–

ANNIE. Bradley!

BRADLEY. No, no…

ANNIE. NO BRAD, FOCUS, now you listen to me. Remember the prize? Remember it? All that money? Your new movie? Remember, give up and all that is gone, okay? Its gonna be fine, now let's do this.

(beat)

BRADLEY. Okay, but–

ANNIE. Good. Open him up.

(**BRADLEY** *picks up the urn and tries to open it.*)

BRADLEY. It won't open…Annie, it won't open.

ANNIE. Try pushing it in and pulling it out like you do on a locker.

BRADLEY. No it's really stuck, I think there might be some sort of suction on the thing.

ANNIE. Righty tighty lefty lucy – c'mon Brad…get it together

BRADLEY. No, seriously it won't open…

ANNIE. Do you have any Vaseline?

BRADLEY. No…

ANNIE. Well, what about soap, because I…

(**BRADLEY** *continues to try to get it to open.*)

BRADLEY. IT'S NOT GONNA OPEN ANNIE, OKAY? It's not, It's just not and I DON'T KNOW WHAT TO DO ANYMORE…I swear to GOD I am going to have a nervous breakdown.

ANNIE. Bradley, that's brilliant, that's a perfect idea! THAT's what we'll do?

BRADLEY. What's what we'll do?

ANNIE. Bradley do you remember in the *Solvits* book four? That BRILLIANT take that you did when you had to pretend to kill yourself to gain respect from the shaman of Yemen so he would hand over his gold?

BRADLEY. So?

ANNIE. *(muttering to herself)* This is perfect – you can stand on the ledge out here…scream I just can't take it anymore, and then I'll call *The Times*–Brad what's the number for *The Times?* Do you remember it?

BRADLEY. I AM NOT GOING TO PRETEND TO KILL MYSELF!!!

ANNIE. Well, you don't actually have to jump!! Don't you see how fantastic this is? We can get the cops and all the people from the press conference out here to talk you down! That should buy us at least like, another week!

BRADLEY. NO!

ANNIE. Bradley, they can't just expect us to reveal the book if you've just attempted suicide. The press will have a field day and while you're sitting in rehab eating *fake* pudding. I can find a computer, bang this out and get that money!

BRADLEY. But what if I fall?

ANNIE. EVEN BETTER!

BRADLEY. WHAT?

ANNIE. Brad, if you break a leg or something, I can refuse to unveil it until YOU recover. It might even be GOOD by the time you get out of the hospital.

BRADLEY. You're crazy; I'm not doing that.

ANNIE. It'll be the greatest performance of a lifetime, Brad!

BRADLEY. But no one will know it's a performance!

ANNIE. I WILL! Listen don't you want to get this movie made?

BRADLEY. I AM not stepping out onto that ledge, it is extremely narrow and scary.

ANNIE. PLEASE?

BRADLEY. NO!

ANNIE. But think of all the presents you'll get…

BRADLEY. I don't want any presents.

ANNIE. Bushes and cartons of flowers you would have…

BRADLEY. What the hell does that mean?!

ANNIE. Oh NEVERMIND, but you'd get TONS of fan mail they might even put you on that rotating news bar you get when you want to sign in to AOL!

BRADLEY. I CANNOT believe I am even discussing this with you anymore…

ANNIE. ITS OUR ONLY OPTION!

BRADLEY. IT'S INSANE! I need a cigarette…

(BRADLEY starts frantically looking under his couch and in the filing cabinet for a cigarette.)

ANNIE. You always say you would DIE for *The Solvit Kids!*

BRADLEY. THAT'S JUST SOMETHING PEOPLE SAY! I'M EXHAUSTED.

(BRADLEY holds his head in his hands. ANNIE goes to comfort him.)

ANNIE. Brad, it's alright…

(She picks him up off the couch and walks him upstage towards the window.)

Breathe, Brad, Breathe,

(BRADLEY is hyperventilating. ANNIE continues to rub his back. BRADLEY is now standing directly in front of the window.)

Maybe if you just, stood on your tip toes and really breathed the air.

(ANNIE nudges him forward a little bit. BRADLEY jumps back.)

BRADLEY. DON'T DO THAT!

ANNIE. CALM DOWN

BRADLEY. YOU WERE GOING TO PUSH ME!

ANNIE. WELL NOT OFF THE LEDGE!

BRADLEY. WHAT DO YOU MEAN NOT OFF THE LEDGE?!

ANNIE. WELL JUST YOUR TIPPY TOES, JUST ENOUGH TO MAKE IT SEEM LIKE A PLAUISIBLE ATTEMTED SUICIDE!

BRADLEY. I COULD HAVE DIED!

(BRADLEY starts to back away from ANNIE. ANNIE follows him.)

ANNIE. NO BUT ITS SUPPOSED TO LOOK CONVINCING THAT'S THE POINT!

BRADLEY. I WOULD QUALIFY THAT AS RECKLESS BEHAVIOR!

ANNIE. IM SORRY I JUST COULDN'T THINK OF ANYTHING ELSE – and you seemed kind of afraid, so–

BRADLEY. YOU TRIED TO KILL ME!

ANNIE. I DID NOT TRY TO KILL YOU, I–

BRADLEY. ANNIE I AM VERY FRAZZLED RIGHT NOW!

ANNIE. BRAD we have no time! AND we have NOTHING to write with!!!

BRADLEY. I'LL GET US SOMETHING TO WRITE WITH!!

*(**BRADLEY** hastily grabs the urn and starts banging it on the floor. The phone rings again.)*

(to phone) Mr. Himmelman what is it? WHAT DO YOU WANT? YES YES, I KNOW, I KNOW IT'S LOUD, I KNOW WE'RE BANGING, I KNOW, I REALIZE, BUT – NO, PLEASE MR. HIMMELMAN DON'T CALL THE POLICE, WE'LL STOP, I JUST–

ANNIE. NOOOO – THAT'S GOOD! TELL HIM TO CALL THE POLICE!!

BRADLEY. *(to **ANNIE**)*: I AM NOT GOING TO KILL MYSELF ANNIE! *(to phone)* WHAT? NO NO – NOT YOU MR. HIMMELMAN! YES I UNDERSTAND WE ARE BEING TOO LOUD FOR YOU BUT WE ARE DEALING WITH A BIT OF A – SHUT UP! MR. HIMMELMAN SHUT UP! I DON'T CARE IF WE ARE BEING TOO LOUD OR IF YOU'RE OLD, I DON'T CARE WHAT I CLOGGED, I DON'T CARE THAT IT'S NIGHT… ALRIGHT FINE FINE I DON'T CARE I CLOGGED THE INCINERATOR, I DON'T CARE, I DON'T CARE, LEAVE ME ALONE, GO BACK TO YOUR WIFE, I CANNOT HANDLE THE–

ANNIE. What did he say?

BRADLEY. I DON'T CARE WHAT HE SAID! *(to phone)* MR. HIMMELMAN YOU ARE A TERRIBLE PERSON AND I WOULD LIKE TO ADD THAT–

ANNIE. Bradley did he say you clogged the incinerator?

BRADLEY. ANNIE DO NOT TOY WITH MY AT THIS MOMENT IN TIME!

ANNIE. What did you clog the incinerator with?

BRADLEY. WHO CARES?

ANNIE. BRADLEY WHAT DID YOU CLOG THE INCINERATOR WITH?

BRADLEY. Oh. *(beat) (to phone)* Uh, Mr. Himmelman what exactly did I clog the incinerator with? A story about a faggot and a shiksa saving Asian people from the navy? And what's the title– ? Right, I see.

ANNIE. Huh.

BRADLEY. Huh.

ANNIE. Tell him we'll be right down–

BRADLEY. *(to phone)* We'll be right down, Mr. Himmelman.
(beat)

ANNIE. And just in time for supper.

THE END